Jekyll and Heidi

R.L. Stine

D1394550

Hippo

Scholastic Children's Books
Commonwealth House, 1–19 New Oxford Street, London WC1A 1NU, UK
a division of Scholastic Ltd
London ~ New York ~ Toronto ~ Sydney ~ Auckland
Mexico City ~ New Delhi ~ Hong Kong

First published in the USA by Scholastic Inc., 1999
First published in the UK by Scholastic Ltd, 1999

Copyright © Parachute Press, Inc., 1999
Goosebumps is a trademark of Parachute Press, Inc.

ISBN 0 439 01183 3

Typeset by Rowland Phototypesetting Ltd, Bury St Edmunds, Suffolk
Printed by Mackays of Chatham plc, Chatham, Kent

10 9 8 7 6 5 4 3 2 1

I stared at the bus ticket in my hand and read my name over and over: Heidi Davidson. Heidi Davidson. Heidi Davidson.

I gazed at it until the words blurred in front of my eyes.

That's how I feel, I thought sadly. I feel like a blur. My life was all bright colours. But now . . . now my future is a grey, mysterious blur.

I know. I know. That sounds like something I read in a book.

But that's the way I think sometimes. I write poetry. Long, sad poems. And I write in my diary every day.

Sometimes I wish I didn't have so much to write about.

I still can't talk about what happened without tears burning my eyes. Growing up in Springfield, my first twelve years were normal and happy.

I have wonderful memories. I don't want to

lose them. I hope my diary will help me remember them for ever.

Then last month, the first part of my life came to an end.

I might as well just say it. My parents . . . they were killed in a horrible car accident.

You can't imagine the shock of it. The days of crying . . . the questions that repeated and repeated in my mind.

Why?

Why did it happen?

Sometimes I felt too overwhelmed by sadness to get out of bed. And sometimes I found myself feeling angry — angry at my parents for leaving me alone.

Where will I live now? I wondered.

Who will I be? Will I still be me?

We have such a small family.

I was sent to live with my only uncle, Dr Palmer Jekyll. He and my aunt are divorced. He lives with his daughter, my cousin Marianna, outside a small village in northern Vermont.

My parents and I visited Uncle Jekyll only once, when I was five. I don't remember much about that visit.

I remember Uncle Jekyll's dark, old house, an enormous mansion. I remember long halls. Big, empty rooms with chairs and sofas covered by dusty sheets.

I remember the bubbling, churning equipment in my uncle's lab — electrical coils, tangles of wire, shelves of glass tubes.

He's a scientist. I don't know what kind.

I remember his stern face, his skin so pale I could almost see the bone underneath it. His cold grey eyes. His long, bony hands on my shoulders, guiding me out of the lab. Gently but firmly.

"This is not a place for you, Heidi." I remember his voice, strangely high and soft, a whisper.

And what did I say to him as he led me out of his lab?

What did I say that made him laugh so hard?

Oh, yes. I raised my round, five-year-old face to him and asked, "Are you *Frankenstein*?"

He laughed so hard, a high, choking laugh. And then he told my parents, and they laughed too.

My cousin Marianna was the only one who didn't laugh.

She was five too, so shy she barely spoke a word. I remember thinking how pretty she was, with her big brown eyes and curly black hair down to her shoulders.

With my straight light brown hair and green eyes, I felt so drab and colourless next to her.

Marianna stayed in her room a lot. When she spent time with us, I found her staring at me.

3

Studying me as if I were some kind of strange zoo animal.

Why didn't she want to talk to me?

Didn't she like me?

These are some of the questions I asked myself as the bus bounced north along the narrow Vermont highway, taking me to my new life.

Outside my window, golden beams of sunlight shot through the tall, snow-covered pines. There are no billboards allowed on the roads in Vermont. It's so pretty and uncluttered here, I thought.

No billboards. And not many cars.

I sighed. I hope it isn't too boring at Uncle Jekyll's. . .

The bus curved sharply along the narrow road. The old woman sitting in front nearly fell out of her seat. She and I were the only passengers.

Behind the endless trees, I saw a small river that followed the road. Sunlight sparkled on its frozen surface.

My face pressed against the glass, I gazed out at the glistening light. The hum and bounce of the bus, the light on the icy river — it kind of hypnotized me.

I didn't realize when the bus stopped. Blinking hard, I turned to the front. The old woman had vanished!

4

My mouth dropped open in surprise. Then I saw the open bus door and realized she had climbed out.

The driver, a big, sweaty, round-faced man, poked his head round. "Shepherd Falls," he announced. "Everybody out."

Everybody out? That was a bit strange since I was the only passenger. I pulled on my blue anorak, tugged my rucksack from the overhead rack, and made my way to the front.

"Is someone meeting you?" the driver asked.

I nodded. "My uncle."

He squinted at me. "No bags?"

"I sent them on ahead." I thanked him and stepped out into the sunlight and cold, fresh air. Sweet-smelling. Piney.

I turned to the bus station, a tiny white-painted shack. No cars in the small car park. A sign over the narrow glass door read: GATE ONE.

I chuckled. The building was much too small for a GATE TWO.

Hoisting my rucksack on to one shoulder, I made my way into the building. My back and leg muscles ached from the long ride. I tried to stretch as I walked.

"Uncle Jekyll?" I was so sure he'd be waiting inside, I called out to him.

But no. No one in the tiny station.

My heart started to pound. My hands felt cold and wet.

5

Take it easy, Heidi, I instructed myself.

Who *wouldn't* be nervous starting a whole new life with people you don't know in a tiny village far from home?

The ticket window at the far wall was closed. Two long wooden benches stretched in the centre of the room. No one sitting there. Someone had left a newspaper on the floor beside the front bench.

Uncle Jekyll knew I was coming, I told myself. So where is he?

What kind of a welcome is this?

I started to cough. Probably from the dust in the station. I'm very allergic to dust. My cough echoed around the empty room.

I turned and hurried back outside. Had Uncle Jekyll pulled into the car park?

No. No sign of him.

"I don't believe this!" I muttered to myself.

Shielding my eyes from the sun, I spotted a pay phone on the side of the station. I'd better try calling him, I decided. I dropped a coin into the slot and punched in the number for Directory Enquiries.

The operator had a New England accent.

"I'd like the number of Dr Palmer Jekyll," I told her. I spelled Jekyll for her.

She mumbled something. I heard the rattle of keyboard keys.

"I'm sorry, dear," she announced. "That number is private. It's unlisted."

"But I'm his niece!" I protested. To my surprise, the words came out shrill and frightened.

"We're not allowed to give the number out," the operator replied gently. "I'm really sorry."

Me too, I thought bitterly. I hung up the phone.

A shadow swept over me. I jumped.

Just a bird. Some kind of blackbird, flying low over the station. I watched it land on the low fence that stretched behind the station. It fluttered its blue-black wings and tilted its head, watching me.

I searched the car park again. Empty. The straight, snow-covered road leading to the station also stood empty.

"Where *is* he?" I asked out loud. "Where?"

"Where is *who*?" a voice demanded.

7

"Huh?" I uttered a startled gasp and spun round.

I stared at a dark-haired boy about my age. He wore a brown sheepskin jacket, open to reveal a blue-and-white ski sweater pulled down over baggy jeans.

"Thank goodness!" I cried. "I thought you were the bird!"

The boy squinted at me. "Excuse me?"

I pointed to the fence. The blackbird had vanished.

I felt myself blushing. "There was a bird on the fence, and I thought it talked to me." As soon as I said it, I knew I was just making things worse.

A gust of wind ruffled the boy's thick brown hair. A smile spread over his face. "We have a lot of talking birds here. We're known for that."

We both laughed. I was starting to feel a little better.

"Are you waiting for someone?" he asked.

I nodded. "My uncle was supposed to pick me up." I glanced down the snowy road. Not a single car had passed since I arrived.

"You got off the bus?" the boy asked. He looked behind me. I think he was searching for my suitcases.

"I'm from Springfield," I told him. "I have to move here. Because . . . well. . ." My voice trailed off.

He introduced himself. His name was Aaron Freidus. I told him my name.

Another gust of wind shook powdery snow from the trees. I pulled my anorak hood up around my head. "Aren't you in school or something?" I asked.

"It's Christmas holidays," he replied. He kicked a clump of snow. "No school."

"Are you waiting for a bus?" I asked.

He laughed. "That would be a long wait. We only get two buses a week."

"Then you just hang out here because it's so exciting?" I teased.

Aaron grinned at me. He had a really nice smile. Actually, he was kind of cute.

He pointed to the station. "My mum works on the counter at the café. On the other side of the station. I'm just waiting for her to get off work."

I gazed over his shoulder at the road,

watching for Uncle Jekyll's car. "Have you lived in Shepherd Falls all your life?" I asked.

He nodded.

"Well . . . what do you do for fun?"

He shrugged. "You can go ice-skating on the river. Do you like to ice-skate? And there's a cinema in Conklin. That's only thirty kilometres away."

Oh, wow, I thought. The only cinema is thirty kilometres from here!

"Do you have cable?" I asked. *Please, please — say you have cable here.*

"No. But a few people have satellite dishes." He sighed. "Most people can't afford them. You know, people in the village are kind of poor."

The late afternoon sun faded behind a cloud. The air grew even colder.

"I think my uncle forgot about me," I said, frowning. "Is there a taxi or something? How do I get to his house?"

"Who is your uncle?" Aaron asked.

"Dr Palmer Jekyll."

Aaron uttered a startled gasp. His dark eyes grew wide. "Heidi!" he cried. "You're not really going to the Jekyll house — are you? Dr Jekyll — he . . . he's a *monster*!"

I laughed.

Aaron looked so funny with his mouth open and his eyes popping out. Like a character in a comic book.

"Give me a break," I said.

"But — but — Dr Jekyll—" Aaron sputtered.

"I know, I know. Jekyll and Hyde," I said, shaking my head. "Dr Jekyll drinks a potion and turns into Mr Hyde, a hideous beast. Everyone knows that old story."

"But, Heidi—" Aaron protested.

"It's just a story. It isn't real," I insisted. "Can you imagine how many awful jokes my poor uncle has probably had to put up with — all because his name is Jekyll?"

"Listen to me! You don't understand!" Aaron screamed.

I took a step back. Why was he suddenly getting so intense?

"Just be quiet for a moment," he demanded,

breathing hard. "It isn't a joke, Heidi. Some kind of frightening beast has been attacking the village. And it —"

"Give me a hint," I interrupted. "Is he big and green, and his name is Godzilla?"

I caught the hurt expression on Aaron's face, and I felt bad about my joke. "You're serious — aren't you?" I asked.

He nodded.

With the sun behind clouds, the snow-covered ground had darkened to grey. Long shadows stretched over the car park.

I suddenly had the strange feeling that I was in an old black-and-white film.

I have feelings like that sometimes. I'm a poet, remember?

"There's an ugly creature," Aaron continued, his eyes locked on mine. "It terrorizes the village. I mean, it runs wild. It wrecks houses and shops. And it hurts people."

"What does that have to do with Uncle Jekyll?" I asked.

Aaron swallowed. "A lot of people here in the village believe your uncle is responsible."

"Huh?" I narrowed my eyes at him. "You're saying my uncle is some kind of . . . creature?"

"He might be," Aaron replied, his voice growing shrill. "Or he might have created the creature. He's a scientist, right? Maybe . . . maybe he's a *mad* scientist! Maybe he was up in his mansion doing evil experiments, and—"

"Enough!" I cried. I turned and walked away. "I know what you're doing, Aaron. It's the old let's-scare-the-new-girl gag." I turned back to him angrily. "But I'm not falling for it. *No way* I'm going to believe such a stupid story."

Again, the hurt expression creased his face. "His name is Jekyll, right?" he asked softly. "Maybe he's a great-great-grandson of the original Dr Jekyll. Maybe—"

"But that's just a *story*!" I cried. "Do you know the difference, Aaron? There's *fiction* — and there's *non-fiction*. Dr Jekyll is *fiction*."

"But the monster is *real*," he insisted. "Everyone in the whole county is afraid to go out at night. We only have four police officers in the village. They don't know what to do."

"They should stop watching scary films at night," I joked. "Then they wouldn't have these nightmares."

"Fine. Okay," Aaron snapped angrily. "Don't believe me. Make jokes. But you should know this, Heidi. The villagers want your uncle arrested. The police just haven't been able to find enough proof."

"How do you know so much about the police?" I demanded.

"My cousin Allan is on the force," he replied. "Besides, it's a small village. Everyone knows everything around here. Even the kids."

13

I stared hard at him, studying his face. He seemed sincere with this monster story. But of course it was a joke. It had to be.

I shivered. "I've got to get to Uncle Jekyll's." I sighed. "Is there a taxi?"

He shook his head. "You can walk there. It's only about twenty minutes or so from here."

"Point me in the right direction," I said.

He pointed to the road. "Just follow it. It goes up through the trees. Up a pretty steep hill. But the street was ploughed this morning. The snow won't be a problem. Your uncle's house is at the top of the hill."

I squinted at the trees, heavy with snow. "Does the house have a street number or anything?"

"No," Aaron replied. "But you can't miss it. It's a huge mansion. It looks like an evil castle in an old horror film. Really."

"Yes, I kind of remember it," I said. Then I had an idea. "Can you walk me there? Can you come with me?"

Aaron lowered his eyes to the ground. "I . . . can't," he murmured. He grabbed my arm. "Please, Heidi. You understand, right? I don't want to die."

I knew Aaron was kidding me. I knew his whole story had to be some kind of joke. But why did I see so much fear in his eyes?

Was he just a good actor?

"Well, maybe I'll see you around," I said. "You know. In town. Or in school."

"Yeah. Catch you later." He turned and ran towards the bus station. He glanced back at me once, then disappeared round the back.

He's probably hurrying to tell his mum about the joke he played on the new girl in town, I decided. The two of them are probably laughing their heads off now.

I took a deep breath, tightened my anorak hood over my head, and started walking. The hard-packed snow crunched under my Doc Martens. Glittering snow-drops fell from the trees, silvery in the late afternoon sun.

"What a horrible day," I murmured. First, Uncle Jekyll doesn't show up. Then I meet a kid who just wants to terrify me with a stupid joke about how my uncle is a monster. Then I have to walk all the way to his house in the freezing cold.

The narrow road sloped up a low hill through the village. I studied the small shops. A barbershop with a snow-covered barber pole, a general store, a tiny post office with a fluttering flag over the door, a gun shop with a display of hunting rifles filling the window.

This is it, I realized. The whole village. Just two blocks long.

A snowy side street curving up from the main road had rows of little houses on each side. They looked like tiny boxes, one after another.

I wondered if Aaron lived in one of those houses.

I leaned into the gusting wind and followed the road up the hill. As I left town, the woods began again. The tree branches creaked and groaned, shifting in the breeze. I heard small animals scuttling over the ground. Squirrels, I thought. Or maybe racoons.

The road curved sharply. I still hadn't passed a single person or car. My rucksack bounced on my shoulders as I climbed.

"Oh." I uttered a sharp cry as Uncle Jekyll's house suddenly came into view. The house — it *did* look like an evil castle from an old horror film.

16

Wet snow-drops from the trees blew into my eyes, blurring my vision. I wiped the snow away and stared up at the enormous dark stone mansion.

My new home.

A sob escaped my throat. I quickly swallowed it.

You're going to be fine, Heidi, I told myself. Don't start feeling sorry for yourself before you even give it a chance.

"It's an adventure," I murmured out loud.

Yes. I planned to think of my new life as an adventure.

My eyes on the house, I trudged up the steep hill. My shoes slipped in the wet snow. The wind swirled around me, roaring louder as I approached the top.

A few minutes later, I stepped into the shadow of the house. The sun seemed to disappear. I blinked in the blue-grey darkness.

And made my way on to the stone steps that led to the black wooden door. I pushed the doorbell.

Why was I shaking all over? From the cold?

I brushed wet snow-drops from the front of my anorak and pushed the doorbell again.

And waited. Waited. Trembling. Breathing hard.

Finally, the heavy door creaked open.

17

A head poked out. A pretty girl's face ringed by long black curls.

Marianna!

"Hi—" I started.

But I didn't get another word out.

"Get away from here!" she whispered furiously. *"Get away while you can!"*

"Huh?" I gasped and nearly fell off the stone steps. "Marianna — what do you mean?"

Her dark eyes flashed. She opened her mouth to reply.

But she suddenly stopped.

I heard the click of footsteps approaching on the wooden floor. Marianna turned back to the house.

A maid in a black uniform and white apron appeared. "It's my cousin Heidi," Marianna explained to the young woman.

The maid laughed. "Well, Marianna, aren't you going to let her in?"

Marianna narrowed her eyes at me, as if warning me again. Then her face went blank, no expression at all. She pulled open the heavy door and motioned for me to enter.

"This is Sylvia," Marianna said, pointing to the maid. "She will help you unpack."

"Your bags arrived two days ago," Sylvia said. "Did you walk from the station?"

I nodded. I still had my anorak hood up. I tugged it down and started to unzip my coat.

"I reminded Dad this morning that you were coming," Marianna said, shaking her head. "He probably forgot."

"You must be frozen," Sylvia said, taking my coat. "I'll make something hot to drink." She hurried away, her shoes clicking on the floor.

I glanced around. Marianna and I stood in a dark hall. High overhead, a large glass chandelier cast pale light that hardly seemed to reach the floor. The walls were papered dark green. The aroma of roasting meat filled the room.

I turned to Marianna. She was tall, at least fifteen centimetres taller than me, and thin. Her black curls flowed down behind a heavy red-and-white check ski sweater. She wore black leggings that made her look even taller.

Again — seven years later — I felt pale and colourless standing next to her.

She crossed her arms over the front of her sweater and led me into a large living room. A fire blazed in a stone fireplace at one end. Heavy brown leather furniture faced the fireplace.

Enormous paintings of snowy-peaked mountain landscapes covered one wall. The curtains were pulled halfway over the front window, allowing in only a narrow rectangle of light.

"How *are* you?" I asked my cousin, forcing some enthusiasm.

"Okay," she replied flatly.

"Are you on holiday from school?" I asked.

She nodded. "Yeah." Her arms were still crossed tightly in front of her.

"How is Uncle Jekyll?" I tried.

"Okay, I suppose," she replied, shrugging. "Really busy."

Marianna is as shy as ever, I decided.

But then I asked myself: Is she shy — or unfriendly?

I kept trying to start a conversation. "Where *is* Uncle Jekyll? Is he at home?"

"He's working," Marianna replied, moving to the window. "In his lab. He can't be disturbed." She turned her back to me and stared out at the snow.

"Well . . . shouldn't I tell him I'm here?" I asked. I picked up a small blue glass bird. Some kind of hawk. I needed something to do with my hands. The glass bird was surprisingly heavy. I set it back down.

Marianna didn't answer my question.

"I walked through the village," I said. "It's pretty tiny. What do you do for fun? Where do you hang out? I mean . . . there *are* other kids our age, right?"

She nodded, but didn't reply. The grey light

21

flooding in from the window made her look like a beautiful statue.

When she finally uncrossed her arms and turned to me, she had the coldest expression on her face. Cold as stone.

"Want to see your room?" she asked.

"Yes. Definitely!" I replied. I followed her to the front stairway. I slid one hand over the smooth black banister as we made the steep climb.

Marianna is just very shy, I decided. She must feel so weird, having a total stranger, someone her own age, move in with her.

"I — I hope we can be like sisters," I blurted out.

A strange, sniggering laugh escaped her lips. She stopped on the stairs and turned back to me. "Sisters?"

"Well . . . yeah," I replied, my heart suddenly pounding. "I know this must be kind of hard for you. I mean—"

She sneered. "Kind of hard? You don't know *anything*, Heidi."

"What do you mean?" I demanded. "Tell me."

She swept her black curls back over her shoulders and continued climbing. We reached the second floor.

I stared up and down an endless passage of darkly flowered wallpaper. The air felt cold and damp. Lights on torch-shaped wall sconces cast a pale glow down the passage. Most of the doors were closed.

"That's my room there," Marianna said, pointing. It appeared to be a mile away at the end of the corridor. She pushed open a heavy door. "And this is your room."

I shut my eyes as I stepped inside. I knew it was going to be gross. Dark and depressing.

When I opened my eyes, I smiled in surprise. "Not bad," I murmured.

The room was totally cheerful. Afternoon sunlight poured in through airy, light curtains on two large windows. I quickly took in a single bed with my suitcases opened on it, a little wooden desk, a chest of drawers, two modern-looking chairs.

Not bad at all.

One wall had floor-to-ceiling bookshelves jammed with books.

Marianna stood in the doorway watching me. "You'll probably want to take Dad's old books out and put your own stuff on the shelves," she said.

"No. I like books," I replied. "Did my computer arrive? And my CD player?"

"Not yet," Marianna replied.

I moved to the window, pushed the curtains aside, and peered out. "What a great view!" I exclaimed. "I can see all the way down the hill to the village!"

"Thrills," Marianna muttered.

I turned to face her. "Are you in a bad mood or something?"

She shrugged. "Sylvia will help you unpack your suitcases, if you want."

"No. I want to do it myself," I replied. I walked to a door next to the chest of drawers. "Is this the wardobe?"

I didn't wait for her to answer. I pulled open the door and stared into an endlessly long wardrobe with shelves and poles on both sides.

"Wow!" I exclaimed. "This is awesome! This wardrobe is almost as big as my whole room back home!"

Back home. . .

The words caught in my throat. I was surprised by the wave of emotion that swept over me.

Tears brimmed in my eyes, and I quickly wiped them away.

I leaned into the wardrobe so Marianna wouldn't see me cry. Get over it, Heidi, I scolded myself. *This* is your home now.

But I wasn't over it.

I wasn't over the tragedy that had changed my life, that had brought me to this strange house in this tiny New England village.

I'll *never* get over it, I thought bitterly, picturing my parents' smiling faces.

I took a couple of deep breaths. Then I

stepped out of the wardrobe. "Marianna, this wardrobe is really —"

She wasn't there. She had vanished.

"What is her *problem*?" I asked out loud.

I moved to the bed and started pulling T-shirts and tops from the first suitcase. I carried them to the chest and began piling them in a drawer. The chest smelled a little mildewy. I hoped my clothes wouldn't pick up the smell.

I filled up the first drawer, then stopped. I really should say hi to Uncle Jekyll, I decided. I really should let him know that I've arrived.

Tugging down the sleeves of my sweater, I hurried out into the hall and made my way to the steps. My heart started to pound. I hadn't seen Uncle Jekyll since I was five.

Would he be happy to see me? I hope he gives me a warmer welcome than Marianna, I thought nervously.

"Heidi — where are you going?"

I turned at the sound of Marianna's voice from down the passage. She poked her head out of her room.

"Down to say hi to Uncle Jekyll," I told her.

"He's in his lab. You really shouldn't disturb him," she called.

"I'll just say hi and then hurry out," I replied.

I ran into Sylvia at the bottom of the stairs. She pointed me in the direction of my uncle's lab.

Down another long corridor. I stopped in front of the lab door.

I raised my hand to knock. But a loud noise on the other side of the door made me jerk my hand back.

It sounded like an animal grunt. A pig, maybe.

I held my breath and listened.

Another pig grunt. Followed by frightening cries. Like an animal caught in a trap. An animal in pain.

I couldn't stand it any longer.

I pushed open the door.

My uncle stood hunched over a long table with his back to me. His long white lab coat came down nearly to the floor.

He dipped his head. And I heard another squeal. Not a human cry. An animal cry.

It's true! I thought, frozen in terror.

He really is acting out the old Jekyll-Hyde story.

Uncle Jekyll drank some weird chemicals. And he turned himself into a terrifying creature!

And then as I stared at him from the doorway, he turned.

Slowly, he turned to face me.

And I uttered a horrified gasp.

I couldn't help myself. My mouth dropped open as I gaped at him.

No. He wasn't a monster.

But Uncle Jekyll looked so old! So much older than how I remembered him.

My mind quickly did the maths. He must be in his early forties, I worked out. But his hair had turned completely white.

He had bags under his red-rimmed eyes and deep, craggy wrinkles down his cheeks. His skin was so pale and dried out, no colour at all, as if he had been sick for a long time.

"Heidi?" he cried out.

He dropped the animal he had between his hands. A guinea pig, I thought. It hit the lab table with a *PLOP*. Then, squealing loudly, it jumped to the floor and scampered across the lab.

"Oh. Sorry," I murmured.

The animal must have been making those grunts and howls, I realized.

The surprise faded from Uncle Jekyll's face, replaced by a smile. "Heidi — you've grown! You've become a young woman! But I'd recognize you anywhere!"

He moved forward and hugged me. His skin smelled of chemicals. His cheek felt dry and scratchy.

When he backed away, his chin was quivering, and his pale grey eyes were wet.

He looks a hundred years old! I thought. What has happened to him?

His smile faded. He slapped his forehead. "I was supposed to pick you up!" he groaned.

"That's okay—" I started.

"I'm so sorry." He shook his head. His long white hair looked as if it hadn't been brushed in weeks! "My work. I'm so involved in the lab. . ."

"A boy at the bus station gave me directions here," I told him. "It was no problem. Really. And Marianna showed me my room."

He sighed. "I've become such a mad scientist, sometimes I work in here for days and lose track of the time."

The equipment chugged and rattled behind him. I saw a wall of cages. Little white creatures, mice and guinea pigs, peered out from some of them.

I heard a long, mournful cry from a room

28

behind the lab. It sounded like the howl of a dog.

"You're doing important work here," I said awkwardly.

He nodded. "Yes. I hope to make a major discovery soon." He sighed again. "But it has been very difficult."

He brushed a hand through the thick tufts of his white hair. His grey eyes studied me for a long moment.

"Is your room okay?" he asked. "We tried to brighten it up, to make it cheerful. This old house is a pretty gloomy place."

"The room is fine," I replied. "Marianna helped me—"

"You will be good for Marianna," Uncle Jekyll interrupted. "Marianna needs someone her age."

"She still seems so . . . quiet," I blurted out.

He nodded. "She is lonely in this big, old house with just her crazy father for company. And I spend so much time on my work. I hope you will not feel neglected, Heidi."

"No. I'll be fine—" I started.

"I hope that you and Marianna. . ." Uncle Jekyll's voice trailed off. He lowered his eyes to the floor.

"I hope so too," I said quickly. "It . . . it's like I'm starting a whole new life here, Uncle Jekyll. And I'm going to try my best to make it great."

He hugged me again. "So much trouble," he murmured. "So much sadness." When he stepped back, his chin was quivering again.

What did he mean?

Was he talking about my parents? About the accident?

Or did he mean something else? Some other kind of trouble?

I headed for the door. But Uncle Jekyll's words reminded me of Aaron. And of the strange story Aaron told me.

I turned back to my uncle. "There *is* something I wanted to ask you about," I said.

Uncle Jekyll had returned to the lab table. He raised his eyes from a thick notebook. "What is it, Heidi?"

"Well. . ." I hesitated. "This boy I met at the bus station. . . He lives in the village. I think he was joking with me. You know. Teasing the new girl in town. But he told me about a beast—"

To my shock, Uncle Jekyll's pale, pale face turned a bright tomato red. "No!" he screamed. "No! *NO!*"

"Huh? I'm sorry!" I choked out, backing towards the door.

Uncle Jekyll's eyes bulged. His face darkened nearly to purple. "There's no beast!" he shrieked. "Don't listen to those crazy stories!" He slammed the table furiously with his fist. "No beast!"

"S-sorry," I stammered again.

I turned and ran out of the lab. A few seconds later, the door slammed behind me.

I stood there in the dark passage, struggling to catch my breath. Uncle Jekyll's angry words rang in my ears. And I couldn't erase the sight of his purple face, his furious eyes, his fist pounding the table.

Why did he totally lose it like that?

Was he telling the truth? If he was, why did he have to scream?

Or did Aaron tell the truth? Did the beast exist? And did it live inside this house?

A hand squeezed my shoulder.

I jumped out of my skin.

I turned to see Sylvia. "I'm sorry," she apologized quickly. "I didn't mean to startle you. Would you like me to help you unpack?"

"No—" I told her. And then I had to tell her what had just happened. "Uncle Jekyll freaked out. I asked him a question, and he started screaming at me."

She nodded and brought her face close enough to whisper, "Your uncle is under a great deal of pressure."

My heart was still pounding. "But he went totally ballistic!" I cried.

"He is a good man," Sylvia said softly. "But his work sometimes drives him over the edge."

I stared hard at Sylvia. What was she trying to tell me?

Over the edge?

What did that mean? That Uncle Jekyll was the beast that Aaron had warned me about?

No. No way.

Calm down, Heidi, I scolded myself. Don't let your imagination run wild.

Sylvia tucked her hands into the pockets of her white apron and led the way up the long staircase to my room. I wanted to unpack by myself. But I let her help me. I didn't feel like being alone.

When we finished, I searched for Marianna. I

knocked on the door to her room. But she didn't answer.

So I explored the old house by myself for a while. Uncle Jekyll's bedroom was a few doors down from Marianna's. I found a small study, crammed with shelves of books on all four walls.

Another small bedroom was neat and cheerful. Probably a guest bedroom, I decided. I wondered if my uncle ever had guests.

Most of the other rooms on the second floor were empty, except for dust and thick cobwebs. A few rooms had furniture covered with old sheets and blankets.

Maybe I can have my own study, I thought. A little den where I can put my CD player and my computer. A place to hang out with my new friends.

New friends. . .

I wished it was term-time. I felt so eager to meet some kids my age.

I moved down the long passage, pulling open doors, exploring. I pulled open the door to a small cupboard — and startled a tiny grey mouse. The mouse stared up at me for a second, then scampered behind a broom.

"Whoa!" I murmured. I shuddered. Are there mice in my room too?

The next room gave me an even bigger scare.

As I pulled open the door, light from the

33

passage swept over the wallpaper — and I gasped.

The room was bare inside, except for two small armchairs, both covered with sheets, standing side by side like ghosts in the middle of the room.

But the dark green wallpaper . . . the walls . . . the walls. . .

They were covered with scratches.

Long, deep scratch marks. Like ruts cut into the walls.

As if some animal had raked its claws over the walls . . . clawed them . . . clawed them . . . until the wallpaper on all four walls stood scratched and shredded.

An animal . . . a creature. . .

I backed out into the hall.

Heard loud breathing.

And realized I wasn't alone.

"Marianna!" I gasped.

Her dark eyes burned into mine. "Heidi, what are you looking at?"

"This room—" I choked out. "The walls. . . They're all scratched. The wallpaper is in shreds. As if. . ." I didn't finish my thought.

Marianna stared at me for a moment longer. Then she turned her eyes away. "George did that," she said softly.

"Huh? George?"

"Our cat. We had a very bad cat," she explained. "He couldn't stand to be by himself. One day, he got locked in this room by accident. And he went crazy."

I peered in at the long scratch marks. They started halfway up the wall.

How could a cat reach up that high?

How could one cat shred all four walls? And make such deep ruts?

"What happened to George?" I asked.

Marianna still had her eyes turned away. "Dad had to put the poor cat to sleep," she replied. "We had no choice. He was just too crazy."

She took my arm. "Come on, Heidi. I came to bring you down to dinner." She smiled for the first time. "A miracle is taking place tonight."

"Huh? A miracle?" I asked, following her down the stairs. "What sort of miracle?"

"Dad is actually joining us. He usually works right through dinner. But tonight, in your honour—"

I stopped her at the bottom of the stairs. "I said something wrong when I saw him," I told her. "I think I made him angry with me."

She raised her dark eyebrows. "Angry? Dad?"

I nodded. "I met a boy at the bus station. His name is Aaron Freidus. Do you know him?"

Marianna nodded. "He goes to my school."

I glanced around the room to make sure Uncle Jekyll wasn't there. "Aaron told me a weird story," I whispered to Marianna. "A very frightening story. About a beast that's been attacking the village."

Marianna gasped and squeezed my arm. Her hand was suddenly ice-cold. "You mentioned that to my dad?"

I nodded. "And then he freaked out."

"He's very sensitive about that," Marianna whispered. "Don't worry. He wasn't angry with you. He gets angry with the villagers. They give him a lot of trouble . . . about his work. He says they make up stories because they are ignorant."

"So Aaron's story isn't true?" I asked.

She made a face. "Of course not."

She let go of my arm and led the way to the dining room. Outside the front window, I saw a bright half moon rising over the bare trees. The tree branches bent and swayed. Wind rattled the old windowpanes.

The dining room was bright and cheerful. A crystal chandelier sent sparkly light down over the long, white-tableclothed table.

Uncle Jekyll was already seated at the head of the table. He had removed his lab coat. He wore a blue denim work shirt over khakis. His thick white hair had been slicked down.

He smiled as Marianna and I entered the room. Then he motioned with his big hands for us to take our seats opposite each other. "Where were you? Heidi, I hope you didn't get lost."

"No. Marianna is a good guide," I said. "But this house would be easy to get lost in," I added.

He patted my hand. "Don't worry. You'll learn your way around quickly."

Sylvia brought in steaming bowls of soup.

"This is real New England clam chowder," Uncle Jekyll said, lowering his head to the bowl and inhaling the steam. "Look at all those clams. Bet you didn't have chowder like this in Springfield."

I laughed. "No. Our chowder came from a tin."

My uncle's good mood, the bright, sparkly room and the wonderful aroma of the creamy, thick chowder were helping to cheer me up.

We had a very pleasant dinner. Uncle Jekyll did most of the talking. Marianna ate silently and only spoke when she was asked a question. But I was beginning to feel a lot more comfortable, a lot more welcome.

As we ate dessert — warm apple pie with vanilla ice cream — Uncle Jekyll recalled my last visit. He told once again the story of how I asked him if he was Frankenstein.

He and I laughed all over again. Marianna ate her dessert silently, eyes lowered.

"You thought I was a mad scientist even then," he said, grinning, his silvery-grey eyes sparkling in the chandelier light. "And, of course, you were right!" he joked.

"If your name is Jekyll, you have no choice," my uncle continued, swallowing a big spoonful of ice cream. "You have to be a mad scientist. People expect it of you. I suppose if I wasn't a scientist—"

"Dad, please—" Marianna interrupted. Bright pink circles had erupted on her cheeks.

She appeared embarrassed by what he was saying.

Uncle Jekyll ignored her. He waved his spoon in the air. "I think the original Dr Jekyll got an unfair deal," he continued. "Everyone thought he was a villain. But Dr Jekyll was actually a brilliant scientist."

I laughed. "A brilliant scientist? I thought he drank stuff that turned him into an evil beast."

Uncle Jekyll nodded. "But you have to be *brilliant* to invent a formula that will change a person so completely. Can you *imagine* finding such an exciting formula?"

"Dad — please!" Marianna begged. "Do we really have to talk about this?"

"Of course we have pills today that change people," he continued. "We have pills to make you sleepy, pills to make you calm. But imagine if someone invented something that completely changed your *whole* personality. That changed you into an entirely different creature! Wow!"

Across the table from mc, Marianna gritted her teeth angrily. "Dad — if you don't change the subject. . ."

"Okay, okay." He raised his huge, bony hands in surrender. "But I still think the original Dr Jekyll was misunderstood."

*

Later that night, I thought about our dinner conversation as I got ready for bed. Why had it upset Marianna so much? I wondered.

At first, she had seemed embarrassed. Then she became angry.

She definitely didn't want her dad to talk about strange formulas that totally changed people. Why not? Because it frightened her?

Or because she knows a secret? A secret about her dad. About the mysterious work he is doing in his lab.

No, Heidi. I scolded myself again. Don't jump to crazy conclusions. Forget about Aaron's stupid story.

I shivered as I pulled on a flannel nightshirt. My room was cold and draughty. But I moved to the window and pulled it open a few centimetres.

Even in the winter I can't sleep with the bedroom window closed. I have to have fresh air.

A cold breeze fluttered the curtains around me. I backed away from them, turned off the lamp on my bedside table, and climbed under the heavy duvet on my bed.

My first night in my new room.

The sheets felt scratchy. And the heavy duvet smelled of mothballs.

Shivering, I pulled the duvet up to my chin and waited to warm up. Silvery moonlight

40

washed in through the window. The curtains fluttered softly.

I shut my eyes and tried to clear my mind.

So much had happened to me. So many changes. So much to think about.

I knew it would take me a long time to fall asleep. No matter how hard I tried, I couldn't shut off my mind.

The faces of my friends back in Springfield floated in front of me. Then I saw my parents, looking so healthy, so happy. I saw my school . . . the house I grew up in. . .

I thought about my bus ride. About Aaron.

About Marianna's strange, unfriendly greeting at the front door. . .

Faces . . . pictures . . . so many words. . .

I was just drifting off to sleep when the terrifying screams began.

I sat straight up, my heart pounding.

Another high, shrill scream.

From right outside my window?

I kicked off the heavy duvet and started to climb out of bed. My legs were tangled in the sheet, and I nearly fell.

The curtains fluttered over me as I dived to the open window and peered out. No one near the house.

The screams were coming from the village.

Gazing down the hill, I saw flashing lights in the town. I heard the wail of sirens, rising and falling. And I saw people running between the houses, running down the main street. Running in small groups.

Dogs barked. I heard a man shouting frantically through a loudspeaker, but I couldn't make out the words.

"It's like a bad dream," I murmured out loud.

I shivered as the cold seeped through my nightshirt. Blown by the strong, steady breeze, the window curtains swirled behind me.

I backed away from the window, the screams and siren wails still in my ears. I hugged myself, trying to warm up.

What is going on down there? I wondered.

My first thought was that a fire had broken out. But I hadn't seen any flames.

And then I remembered Aaron's story. "We're all afraid to go out at night," he told me, his dark, serious eyes burning into mine.

The beast?

Was there really a beast out there?

Uncle Jekyll insisted that the beast didn't exist. He had acted so strangely, becoming so angry when I mentioned it.

If there was no beast, no wild, evil creature that attacked the town — what was happening down there?

My mind spinning, I lurched to my closet. I searched in the dark for my dressing gown.

I'm going downstairs to ask Uncle Jekyll to explain, I decided.

The sirens. The flashing lights. The screaming people running from their homes.

It really is like a bad dream. Except I know I'm awake.

"Aaaagh!" I let out a frustrated cry. I couldn't

find my dressing gown. Had I unpacked it? This new room — this new wardrobe — I didn't know where anything was!

A sob escaped my throat. Will I ever feel at home here? I wondered.

How can I feel at home when there's a *horror film* going on outside my window?

I had tossed my jeans and sweatshirt on the chair beside my chest of drawers. I pulled them on quickly, my hands trembling, and hurried into the passage.

A single ceiling light near Marianna's room at the end of the passage cast a dim circle of light. Squinting until my eyes adjusted, I ran to Uncle Jekyll's room.

The door stood half open. I knocked and called his name.

No answer.

I pushed the door open and peered inside. "Uncle Jekyll?"

No. Not there. The bed was still made. He hadn't come up to sleep yet.

"He must still be in his lab," I murmured to myself. Marianna said that he worked all hours of the night.

I turned and hurried down the stairs. Then I made my way along the back hall till I came to my uncle's lab.

"Uncle Jekyll? Are you in there?"

The door stood open. Pale fluorescent light

washed down from low ceiling lamps, making everything look an eerie green.

I poked my head in. "Uncle Jekyll?"

The equipment bubbled and churned. A row of small red lights on a machine in the corner blinked on and off.

I stepped into the lab. A sharp, sour aroma greeted my nose. On the long lab table, a thick green liquid dripped slowly — one drip at a time — from a high glass tube into a large glass beaker.

"Uncle Jekyll? Are you in here?"

I made my way along the table and peered into the little room behind the lab. No. No sign of him.

I turned to leave. But stopped when my eyes landed on the object at the edge of the table.

A drinking glass. Empty except for a little puddle on the bottom and a green film on the sides.

I swallowed hard and stepped up to examine the glass. I stared into it. Then I sniffed it. It smelled sharp and sour.

"Ugh." I backed away.

The thick green liquid clung to the sides. Was it the same liquid dripping from the glass tube?

Did my uncle drink that stuff?

Did he drink that foul liquid and turn himself into a creature, a wild beast? Was he down in the village now, attacking people, terrifying everyone?

"That's crazy!" I cried. My voice echoed shrilly off the walls of the lab.

The red lights blinked on and off. And the *DRIP DRIP DRIP* of the thick green liquid into the glass beaker seemed to grow louder.

I don't *want* to live in a horror film! I told myself.

I covered my ears with my hands. I couldn't stand the blinking lights, the bubbling, churning and dripping.

I ran out of the lab. Down the back corridor, searching every room for him. The kitchen. The dining room. A study I hadn't seen yet. The living room.

Dark. All dark.

No sign of Uncle Jekyll.

If he wasn't down in the village, terrorizing everyone, *where was he*?

I stopped at the front stairs, breathing hard. I leaned on the smooth wood of the banister, waiting to catch my breath.

And then my entire body went cold — and I froze in fright as the heavy front door creaked and swung open.

I gripped the banister and gaped in silence as Uncle Jekyll staggered into the house.

His white hair shot out wildly around his head, as if it had been shocked with electricity. His pale eyes bulged. His face was smeared with dirt.

He didn't see me. He shut his eyes tight as if he were in pain. He uttered a low groan as he bumped the door closed with his shoulder.

The sleeve of his black overcoat was ripped at the shoulder. His blue work shirt had come untucked from his trousers. Long, muddy smears ran down the front of the shirt. Most of the buttons were missing.

Wheezing loudly, Uncle Jekyll lurched across the front hall. His boots left a trail of muddy prints on the floor. The legs of his trousers were stained, one knee torn.

I gripped the banister tighter. I wanted to disappear. I didn't want him to see me there. I didn't want him to explain where he had been or what he had done.

I didn't want to know.

It was all too terrifying.

"Heidi—"

I shuddered when he rasped my name. I squeezed the banister so hard my hand ached.

"Heidi? What are you doing down here?" he demanded, moving closer, eyeing me warily.

"I — I couldn't sleep," I choked out. "I heard noises. Screams and things."

He tried to push down his hair, but it remained wild and standing straight up. His pale grey eyes searched my face, as if trying to see inside me, to find out what I knew. What I suspected.

"Uncle Jekyll—" I said in a trembling voice. "Where did you go?"

"For a walk," he answered quickly. He scratched his cheek. "I like the air late at night. I often take a long walk around the hill when I have finished my work."

"But your clothes—" I started to protest. "Your face—"

"I fell," he answered quickly. A strange smile spread over his mud-smeared face. "I must look a sight. Sorry if I frightened you, Heidi."

"You . . . fell?" My eyes went to the missing buttons on his shirt, the tear at the knee of his trousers.

He nodded. "The tall grass is so slippery after a heavy frost," he said. "I wasn't watching where I was going. I was foolish. I usually bring my torch, but tonight I forgot it."

"And you fell? Are you hurt?" I asked.

He sighed. "Not too badly. My head hit a low branch. I couldn't see it in the dark." He rubbed his forehead. "I was so startled, I slipped and rolled halfway down the hill."

"That's awful," I declared.

Did I believe him?

I wanted to. I really wanted to.

But I didn't.

He rubbed his forehead some more. His eyes remained locked on me. "Next time I'll remember the torch," he said. "I could have broken my neck."

"I — I heard screams," I stammered. "From the village. I saw lights and heard sirens. I—"

"I don't know what that is," he replied sharply.

"Something bad—" I started. "People were running and—"

"I didn't see anything," he interrupted. "I was walking in the woods. I couldn't see the village. I didn't hear anything."

"It was so frightening," I told him. "The screams woke me up."

He shook his head and rubbed the back of his neck. "I'm so sorry," he murmured. The tenderness in his voice took me by surprise.

"It's your first day here," he continued. "I know how hard this is for you. I know your whole life has been turned upside down, Heidi."

"Yes," I agreed. I lowered my head so he couldn't see the tears brimming in my eyes.

"Give yourself time to adjust," Uncle Jekyll advised, speaking in a whisper. "These tiny New England villages can be a little strange. Try not to pay attention. Try to let things slide for a while. You'll be a lot happier if you do."

Let things slide?

Don't pay attention?

What was he saying? That I should *ignore* the screams and sirens and people running wildly through the town?

I stared hard at him, trying to understand.

He said I'd be a lot happier if I ignored what I heard and saw.

Was that advice from a caring uncle?

Or a threat?

It took a long time to get back to sleep. The excitement had ended down in the town. No more sirens or screams. A few dogs continued to bark. But all else was silent.

I pulled the duvet up high and stared at the ceiling. My mind was spinning with thoughts of all that had happened.

Uncle Jekyll was lying to me. I knew that.

He hadn't fallen down the hill. And he knew very well what had happened in town.

But was he lying to protect me? Or to protect himself?

Finally, I fell into a deep, dreamless sleep.

I slept late. When I awoke and went to the window, the sun was already high over the winter-bare trees. The snow down the hill sparkled brightly. For a brief second, I glimpsed a deer trotting into a thick cluster of pines.

I stretched, smiling as the fresh morning air

floated in through my open window. But my good mood vanished as soon as the frightening memory of the night before swept back into my mind.

I have to know the truth, I told myself.

I won't be able to relax — until I learn the truth about Uncle Jekyll.

I pulled on a clean pair of black leggings and a bright yellow woollen sweater and hurried down to breakfast.

But angry, shouting voices made me stop in the passage outside the kitchen.

"I don't have to stay here!" I heard Marianna cry angrily. "I don't have to live like this!"

"Sure, sure," Uncle Jekyll replied sarcastically. "And where would you go?"

"Anywhere!" she shrieked. "Anywhere where I didn't have to put up with you!"

"Keep your voice down," Uncle Jekyll urged, sounding desperate. "The whole house doesn't have to hear."

"I don't care! I really don't care!" Marianna wailed. "I'm so tired of living with so many lies, so many secrets! I — I can't do it any more, Dad! You're asking too much!"

Leaning against the wall, out of sight of the kitchen door, I clapped my hand over my mouth to keep from gasping.

What was Marianna saying? Did she know the truth about her father?

My heart pounded as I eavesdropped on their argument.

"I can't have any friends," Marianna was saying in a trembling, emotional voice. "I can't invite anyone over. I have no life, Dad. No life at all. And it's all your fault!"

"You have to be patient," Uncle Jekyll replied heatedly. "You have to give me time, Marianna. You know it isn't my fault."

"I don't care!" she shrieked. "I don't care any more!"

Uncle Jekyll started to say something else. But I coughed. I didn't even realize I had done it.

Their argument ended instantly. The kitchen was silent now.

I took a deep breath. Put a blank expression on my face. And tried to act casual as I walked into the room.

Everyone said good morning.

Uncle Jekyll smiled. But Marianna gritted her teeth and glanced away.

Her bowl of cereal hadn't been touched. Her dark curls fell damply over her face. Her hands were clenched into tight fists on the tabletop.

"Would you like some eggs?" Uncle Jekyll asked, the smile plastered on his face. "Sylvia can make them for you any way you like."

"No. I'll just have cereal." I reached across

53

the table for the box. "I'm not a big breakfast person."

"Marianna and I were just having a little family discussion," Uncle Jekyll said, grinning across the table at her.

Marianna scowled and didn't raise her eyes.

"Oh, really?" I said. "I missed it."

No one said much for the rest of breakfast. I couldn't wait to take Marianna aside and find out what she knew. I'm not going to let her go until she tells me everything, I vowed.

After breakfast, Uncle Jekyll disappeared into his lab. He closed the door after him, and then I heard him lock it.

I tracked Marianna down in her room. She was leaning over a small glass cage. She held a cute brown-and-white hamster in her hand.

"Who is that?" I asked, trying to sound cheerful and bright.

"Ernie," Marianna replied, not turning around. The hamster moved from hand to hand. "Ernie is my best friend in the whole world."

"He's cute," I said. I stepped up beside her. "I like his pink nose."

Marianna nodded but didn't reply.

I took a deep breath. I couldn't wait any longer. I had to hear her story.

"I lied this morning," I confessed. "Before breakfast. I heard you and your dad."

She wrapped Ernie in one hand. Her dark eyes flashed. "You did?"

I nodded. "You sounded pretty upset."

Marianna frowned. "We were just talking. You know."

"No, you weren't," I blurted out. "I heard what you were saying. About lies and secrets."

She didn't reply. She narrowed her eyes at me thoughtfully. "No big deal," she murmured.

"Come on, Marianna," I pleaded. "Tell me the truth. I heard the screams from the town last night. From my bedroom window, I can see everything down there. I heard the sirens. I saw the people running."

"I . . . I don't know anything about that," she murmured.

"Yes, you do!" I insisted. "I want to know the truth, Marianna. The truth about your dad. You have to tell me. You have to!"

Marianna staggered back. Her face contorted angrily. "Leave me alone!" she shrieked, breathing hard. "Don't snoop around, Heidi. Don't do it. Don't try to learn about my father. You'll regret it! I'm warning you!"

We both gasped as we looked down at her hand.

"Oh, noooo," she moaned.

She had squeezed the hamster to death.

I have to get away from this house, I decided.

I'd left Marianna sobbing in her room. She refused to listen to my apologies. And slammed her bedroom door in my face as I backed out of the room.

I can't believe she killed her hamster, I thought, shuddering. I can't believe she squeezed it like that.

Now she hates me, I realized. She blames me. Blames me. . .

She didn't like me before. But now she hates me.

Now she'll never tell me what she knows about her dad.

Now she'll never tell me what they were arguing about this morning. About the lies and secrets. . .

I felt so upset. My chest fluttered. My stomach felt as hard as a rock.

"I have to go. . . I have to go," I chanted to myself as I returned to my room.

I pulled on my anorak and looked for my gloves. I pulled out all my drawers and got down on my hands and knees to search the floor of the wardrobe. But I couldn't find them anywhere.

"Forget the gloves," I muttered. "So you'll have cold hands. Get out, Heidi. Get out of the house."

I hurried outside. I had to get away from Marianna and her father. And their creepy, dark mansion. And all of their secrets.

The cold, fresh air made my cheeks tingle. The bright sun, high in a clear blue sky, felt warm on my skin.

I tossed back the anorak hood and shook out my long brown hair. The hard snow crunched under my boots as I made my way along the walk that led to the side of the house.

From here, I could see the narrow road twisting down the hill to town. Only a few patches of snow here and there.

I found an old girl's bike in the garage. It probably belonged to Marianna.

I leaned heavily on the handlebars and tested the tyres. They seemed full enough to carry me.

"Yes!" I cried happily. "Escape!"

A few seconds later, I was riding down the

hill, pedalling hard, the tyres bumping over the unpaved road, my hair flying behind me like a flag.

It felt so good. I wanted to sing and shout.

Above me, I saw Canada geese soaring high in a tight V formation. They honked noisily as they flew past.

Snow-covered pines became a green-and-white blur as I whirred downhill.

I stood up and pedalled, enjoying the exercise, the cool, sweet air, the feeling of freedom.

My good mood lasted until I reached the outskirts of the village.

Then I found myself back in the middle of a horror film.

I slowed my bike as the first house came into view. I gazed at the metal shed behind the house. It lay on its side, one wall smashed in.

"Whoa," I murmured. The log fence around the back garden had a big gap in it. It looked as if it had been ripped apart. Logs were strewn over the snow, broken and bent.

The downstairs windows of the next house were shattered. Shards of glass were scattered over the snow, reflecting the morning sun. A side door had been ripped off its hinges. It tilted against the wall of the house.

It looks as if a tornado has swept through here, I thought.

I pedalled on. I saw a group of men and women standing outside the house on the corner. They huddled around a car in the driveway, talking quietly, shaking their heads.

As I rode nearer, I saw that the car windscreen had been smashed. A million cracks stretched out in the glass like spiders' webs.

The driver's door lay on the driveway beside the car, bent and battered. The steering wheel, wires dangling, poked out from beneath the car.

"What happened?" I called from the street.

The men and women turned to me. "Don't you know?" a woman called.

"Are you new here?" a man asked. "Haven't you heard?"

"Did you crawl out from under a rock?"

They seemed so angry, so unfriendly, I turned the corner and rode on.

"Be careful!" a man called after me. "Don't ride that thing at night!"

The bike tyres crunched over broken glass. Two more cars had had their windscreens shattered.

A black-and-white police car was parked beside a small brick house on the next block. Two grim-faced officers were helping an old man re-attach his front door.

All of the windows in the house were covered with newspaper. Broken glass littered the front garden.

A few seconds later, I turned another corner and found myself on the main street of town. A small crowd had gathered around a red-and-white truck, parked in the middle of the street.

I pedalled closer, then jumped off my bike. I

read the bold letters on the side of the truck: ACTION NEWS 8.

Walking my bike up to the crowd, I saw a man with a video camera on his shoulder. In the centre of the crowd, a young red-haired woman held a microphone.

A TV news crew, I realized. What *happened* here last night?

I pushed through the circle of people. The reporter poked the microphone into a familiar face.

Aaron!

He was talking to the woman, his eyes on the microphone. He didn't see me.

I moved close enough to hear what they were saying.

"And so the beast attacked again last night?" the reporter asked him.

Aaron gazed at the microphone. "Yes. It came running down the hill a little before eleven. And it started tearing things up."

"Were you outside that late? Did you see it come down the hill?" the reporter asked, turning her head and glancing at the snow-covered hill rising over the village.

"Well . . . no," Aaron replied. "I was at home. My parents won't let me go out. My curfew is nine o'clock — because of the beast."

"Have you ever seen this creature?" the woman asked.

A truck rumbled by.

"Cut! Wait for the truck! It's too noisy!" the man with the camera instructed.

They waited for the truck to pass. Then the cameraman signalled for Aaron to talk again.

"What was the question?" he asked.

"Have you ever seen the creature?" the woman repeated. She pushed the microphone up to Aaron's mouth.

"Yes."

"Is it human?"

"Well. . ." Aaron thought hard. "Sort of. It's about the size of a human. And it walks on two legs. Except it kind of staggers. But it's very furry."

"Furry?" the reporter asked.

Aaron nodded. "It has grey fur all over. On its arms. And its back. And it growls like a wolf or something."

"So it's an animal?" the woman asked.

Aaron rubbed his chin. "I'd say it's half-human, half-animal. I'd say—"

"Go up the hill," a woman in the crowd shouted at the reporter. She stepped in front of Aaron and grabbed the microphone. "You want to get your news story? Don't waste your time down here. Go up to the big house up there. Dr Jekyll's house. You want to see the monster? You'll find him in there!"

62

"No, you won't!" I cried. "I live in that house — and there's no monster in there!"

I gasped and clapped my hand over my mouth.

Why did I say that?

Why did I suddenly try to defend Uncle Jekyll?

Why didn't I keep my big mouth shut?

With cries of surprise, everyone turned to stare at me.

"Who is she?" someone asked.

"I've never seen her before," a young man replied.

Aaron narrowed his eyes at me. "Heidi? What are you doing here?" he whispered.

The others stared at me coldly, suspiciously.

I'm in trouble now, I realized.

I'm in big trouble.

"She's a Jekyll? *Get* her!" an angry voice growled.

I gasped and took a step back.

Were they going to attack me?

No. No one moved. They circled me, staring at me so coldly — as if *I* were the beast!

"My uncle isn't a monster!" I cried, my voice trembling. "And there's no monster living in his house."

Did I really believe that?

I didn't know what to believe. But these people didn't know the truth, either.

Why should they accuse Uncle Jekyll when they had no proof?

I took another step back and tripped over my bike. I'd forgotten I'd set it down on the pavement. My heel caught the front wheel, and I fell hard, landing in a sitting position on top of it.

The young woman reporter hurried over and reached out her free hand to help me up. Then she poked the microphone into my face. "Can you take us inside?" she asked eagerly.

I gaped at her. "Excuse me?"

"Can you take us inside your uncle's house? Can you let us see for ourselves?" she demanded.

"Uh . . . well. . ." I hesitated.

"See? She's lying!" a man shouted.

"She's a Jekyll. She's hiding the beast!" a woman cried.

"No . . . my uncle. . ." I stammered. "You have to get my uncle's permission," I told the reporter.

Then I turned to the crowd, my heart pounding, my throat so dry I could barely swallow. "I'm new here!" I cried. "I've just moved here! I . . . I don't know anything!"

No one moved. No one spoke.

They stared so hard at me, as if trying to see inside my head.

They hate me, I thought. They don't even know me, and they hate me.

And then Aaron stepped forward, moving quickly.

His sudden movement startled me. I shrank back, thinking he planned to hurt me.

But he bent down and picked up my bike for me. "Heidi, you'd better go," he whispered. "Everyone in town is really upset. And scared."

"But I—" I started.

"Last night was so terrifying," Aaron whispered. "No one knows what to do." He handed

65

the bike to me. "Hurry. Go back to your uncle's house. You'll be safe there."

Will I? I wondered.

I jumped on the bike and started pedalling away.

Will I be safe there?

I spent a dreary afternoon in the house. Uncle Jekyll never came out of his lab. I searched for Marianna but couldn't find her.

A freezing rain pounded the windows. The house was cold and damp. I pulled a heavy woollen sweater over two T-shirts, but I still felt chilled.

I explored the house for a while, pulling open doors, searching rooms cluttered with old books and magazines.

I poked my head into the room with the scratched walls. I imagined a wild, snarling creature locked in there. I pictured it roaring furiously as it scraped long, curling claws over the walls. Shredding the wallpaper . . . shredding it . . . shredding it.

With a shudder, I backed out of the frightening room and pulled the door shut. I reminded myself not to go back there.

I made myself a sandwich for lunch. Then spent most of the afternoon reading in my room.

A few hours before dinner, a man arrived

from the phone company. Sylvia showed him into my room. I watched happily as he installed a phone on my desk.

"Yessss!" I cried after he left, pumping my fist in the air. I couldn't wait to try my new phone. I was desperate to call my friend Patsy back in Springfield.

"Well, Heidi? How is it?" she demanded after we said hi and how much we missed each other. "How is your new home?"

"Well. . ." I hesitated. I didn't want to tell her how strange and frightening everything was. But I couldn't hold it back. I had to tell someone.

"Patsy — it's awful here!" I cried, checking to make sure my bedroom door was closed. "My uncle Jekyll — he's totally weird. My cousin Marianna is so unfriendly. And there's a creature — some kind of creature that keeps attacking the village. The people here—"

I stopped, breathing hard.

And listened.

What was that clicking sound I kept hearing?

And then I heard breathing.

Not Patsy's breathing.

He's listening in! I realized.

Uncle Jekyll! He's listening on another phone! He's *spying* on me!

"What's that about a creature?" Patsy demanded. "You're kidding — right?"

"H-hold on a minute," I stammered.

I tossed the phone on to my bed and ran out of the room. I flew down the stairs and into the front hall.

Where was Uncle Jekyll? Where?

I wanted to catch him in the act. I wanted to know for sure if he was spying on me.

I spotted him on an armchair in the study. Sitting next to the phone.

As I burst into the room, I saw him pick up a book and pretend to read it. "Heidi? Hi." He pretended to be surprised to see me.

I stared at him, breathing hard, my mouth open.

I'm not safe here, I realized.

I'm trapped. I'm a prisoner here.

A strange smile spread over Uncle Jekyll's face. "Are you enjoying your new phone?" he asked.

The next night, I had a frightening dream. I knew I was dreaming, and I struggled to wake up. But I couldn't escape it.

A creature chased me across a snow-covered field. Growling, raging at the top of its lungs, it staggered after me on its hind legs.

Half-wolf, half-man, it raised its hairy snout to the sky and bellowed. Its red eyes glowed like fire, and thick gobs of yellow saliva ran down its furry chin.

I ran harder, harder. I leaned into a blowing wind and churned my legs, running so hard that every muscle ached.

But my shoes slipped on the snowy surface. It was like running on a treadmill. I ran and ran but didn't move forward.

The beast roared closer. I saw it snap its jagged-toothed jaws. I felt its hot, sour breath on my hair and the back of my neck.

I tried to run harder. Harder. But I wasn't

going anywhere. My shoes slid over the slippery snow.

And then I fell. Facedown.

The creature leaped on top of me.

Its red eyes flamed above me. The thick yellow saliva puddled on my face, steaming hot.

"Nooooooo!" I wailed. I tried frantically to twist away. But it pinned me to the snow. So heavy . . . so heavy I couldn't breathe.

And then the creature opened its jaws. Lowered its head.

And sank its teeth into my shoulder.

I woke up with a sharp gasp.

The beast vanished. The white snow faded to black.

At first, I didn't know where I was. It took a few seconds to remember.

In a strange bed. In a strange room.

I sat up dizzily and rubbed my shoulder. It ached. It felt so sore.

From the dream?

My nightshirt was drenched with sweat. I climbed out of bed and, still shaky, made my way to the chest of drawers. I clicked on the light. Found a clean nightshirt. And changed.

I glanced at the clock. Nearly four in the morning. Dark outside. And silent.

Images of the dream floated back to me. The

70

chase. The horrifying roars of the creature. The hot breath on my neck.

I'll never get back to sleep, I realized. Maybe if I read for a while, I'll get sleepy again.

I took a few deep breaths. "Get over it, Heidi," I told myself out loud. "It was just a dream."

I made my way to the wall of books. Uncle Jekyll's old books. There must be something here to read, I thought. Maybe I can find something really boring that will put me right to sleep.

On a high shelf, I thought I spotted a children's book I'd loved as a kid. I reached for it. But my bare foot caught on the edge of the carpet.

I stumbled forwards. My shoulder bumped into the bookshelf.

"Huh?" As I caught my balance, a board on the side of the shelf dropped down.

I moved over to it. A secret compartment.

I'd knocked open a secret compartment in the bookshelf.

I brought my face close and peered inside.

"Wow," I murmured. "What's hidden in there?"

I reached a hand in and pulled out an object. A book.

It appeared to be very old. It had a brown leather cover. The leather was cracked and crinkly.

I ran a finger over the faded letters on the front: DIARY.

An old diary.

I flipped through the pages. They were yellow and brittle. And covered with words, diary entries written in black ink in a tiny handwriting.

"Weird," I murmured. "Who would hide their diary inside a bookshelf?"

I carried the diary to the chair across from my bed and clicked on the lamp. Then, yawning, I settled into the chair and began to examine it.

I searched for the owner's name on the inside covers and on the first page. But the covers were blank except for yellow-brown age stains. And the first page began with the diary entry for January 1.

What year? What year?

The book didn't say. No owner. No date.

I blew dust off the spine. No information there.

I flipped through the pages again, careful not to tear the brittle paper. Then I opened the book somewhere near the beginning. Squinting at the tiny handwriting, I started to read:

. . .So cold today. The snow coming down in sheets, driven by the howling winds. I know I will howl too. I cannot control it. And I will go out in the storm. Because the storm inside me is more powerful than any snowstorm. . .

"Huh?" I stared at the yellowed page, gripping the little book tightly in my lap.

What was this person writing about? A *storm* inside him?

Was that some kind of poetry?

I turned a few more pages and began reading again:

. . .I know what I did tonight. I remember every scream, every cry of horror. Those poor people. They don't deserve it. They don't deserve *me*.

But I am powerless to control it. At night

73

when the urge comes over me, when my body makes its hideous changes . . . I must go out. What choice do I have?

I must run and rage and howl. And I must *feed*.

I know what I am on those terrifying but exciting nights. I am like a wild beast. And I live for the screams. And for the fear I create. . .

"Whoa!" I murmured. My heart pounded in my chest.

Wind rattled the windowpanes. I pulled the duvet from the bed over my chair and snuggled under it.

I started to read another page:

. . .Of course I am a human most of the time. A caring, frightened human. A human prisoner in this old house. And a prisoner in this body that changes at night. A prisoner in this body I cannot control.

Where does the rage come from? From where does the anger spring — the anger that forces me to kill and destroy? There are two of us trapped here. Two prisoners . . . the beast and the doctor. . .

The doctor?

I stared at the tiny handwriting, reading

those words again and again until they blurred in front of my eyes.

The beast and the doctor. . .

Trapped in one body?

I shut the diary and studied the worn leather cover. Was I holding the diary of the *original* Dr Jekyll?

Dr Jekyll, who drank the potion and became the hideous, twisted, dangerous Mr Hyde?

But how can that be? I asked myself, gripping the little book tightly.

Dr Jekyll wasn't real — was he?

And then other questions flooded my mind. . .

Did my uncle find this diary? Did Uncle Jekyll hide the diary in the secret compartment?

Did Uncle Jekyll study the old diary? Did he learn the original Dr Jekyll's horrible secrets?

Has my uncle turned himself into a monster?

So many questions!

I didn't have time to think about answers.

I heard footsteps in the hall — and then my bedroom door swung open.

I tried to shove the diary under the duvet. "Uncle Jekyll?" I gasped.

No. No one there.

I realized the breeze from the passage had swung the door open. I let out a long sigh of relief.

Shoving the duvet away, I climbed unsteadily to my feet. I flipped quickly through the diary, searching for the secret formula. No. No sign of it.

I carried the diary to the bookshelf and placed it carefully in its hiding place.

Then I closed the secret compartment, turned off the lights, and climbed into bed. I shut my eyes, but the tiny handwriting, the frightening words, still danced in front of my eyes.

The beast and the doctor. . .

Did Uncle Jekyll find the formula for the original Dr Jekyll's potion? Was it hidden somewhere in the diary? Did he follow the directions and mix it himself?

And drink it?

Was my uncle the beast that was terrifying Shepherd Falls?

I couldn't stay here if he was.

I was in terrible danger.

I had to learn the truth — fast.

But how?

Lying in bed, tossing from side to side, wide awake, I thought of a plan.

I waited until after dinner the next night. Then I hid in Uncle Jekyll's lab.

I found the lab door closed. I turned the knob, pulled the door open, and crept inside.

The equipment churned and bubbled. On the long lab table, I saw two glass beakers half-filled with a purple liquid. A clear liquid dripped from a glass tube into a gallon-sized bottle.

Uncle Jekyll and Marianna were still at the dinner table. We'd had a quiet — almost silent — dinner. Marianna kept casting angry glances at her father. Uncle Jekyll pretended to ignore them.

"Are you going out tonight?" he asked her.

An odd question. I'd never seen Marianna leave the house.

"I don't know what I'm doing," she mumbled into her tuna casserole.

I asked to be excused, saying I didn't want any dessert.

I knew I had very little time to hide. My

uncle always headed straight for his lab after dinner.

My eyes searched the long, cluttered room. Where could I hide? Where could I hide safely but still be able to spy on Uncle Jekyll?

A row of dark metal cabinets across from the lab table caught my eye. They looked like the hall lockers at my old school.

I darted over to them and began pulling open the doors one at a time. The narrow cabinets were all jammed with equipment. No room for me.

I heard Uncle Jekyll's voice out in the hall. He was arguing again with Marianna.

I searched desperately for a hiding place.

I'm going to be caught! I realized. He'll ask me what I'm doing in here. And I won't have an answer.

My heart thudding in my chest, I pulled open the last cabinet door. Yes! Only a few towels on the bottom.

I took a deep breath and squeezed inside. I pulled the metal door nearly closed — just as Uncle Jekyll stepped into the lab.

Peering through the narrow opening, I held my breath. Did he see me swing the door shut? Could he hear my heart pounding like a bass drum?

He moved to the table and inspected the beakers with the purple liquid.

He didn't see me, I realized. I slumped against the back of the closet and slowly let my breath out.

He poured the purple liquid carefully into a rack of slender glass test tubes. Then he adjusted some dials on the electronic equipment at the end of the table.

What is he working on? I wondered.

He is working so fast, so urgently. He must be in his lab at least twenty hours a day.

Why is he working so hard? What is he trying to do?

I hope it is something *good*, I prayed. I hope his work has nothing to do with the creature that is wrecking the village.

Maybe he's trying to cure a disease, I told myself. Maybe he's very close. He has almost found the cure. And he is working day and night because he knows he almost has it.

Or maybe he is in a race with another doctor. Uncle Jekyll wants to cure the disease before the other doctor beats him to it.

I desperately wanted my uncle to be *good*. I didn't want him to be a mad scientist. An evil villain. A . . . creature.

Please . . . I prayed. . . Please don't drink your formula and turn into a growling beast. Please . . . let the people in the town be wrong about you.

I watched as his hands moved furiously over the table. Pouring clear liquids into purple liquids. Turning knobs and dials. Mixing chemicals from one test tube to another. Holding glass beakers over a flame until the liquid inside bubbled and steamed.

Electricity sizzled over the table. Uncle Jekyll kept shocking the dark liquid in a beaker with some sort of electric probe.

His head bent, his shoulders slumped under the white lab coat, he worked feverishly, without ever stopping for a second, without coming up for air.

I began to feel cramped in the narrow cabinet. My knees ached. My back ached. Pressed against the metal sides, my arms had fallen asleep.

This was a big mistake, I decided. I'm not going to see anything interesting at all. I should have trusted Uncle Jekyll. I shouldn't be hiding in here spying on him.

I watched him raise a test tube to the fluorescent light over the table. It contained a rust-coloured liquid that glowed in the light.

He studied it for a moment, turning it between his fingers.

Then he tilted back his head. Lowered the test tube to his mouth.

And drank the liquid down.

Oh, no, I thought, feeling heavy dread knot

my throat. I pressed a hand over my mouth to keep from crying out.

Uncle Jekyll licked his lips. Then he raised another test tube with a green liquid inside — and poured that down his throat too.

He swallowed noisily and licked his lips.

Then he braced himself. He flattened both hands on the tabletop and leaned forward. As if waiting for the liquids to do something to him.

I stared through the narrow opening. I couldn't breathe. I couldn't move.

Leaning hard against the tabletop, Uncle Jekyll shut his eyes. His mouth twisted. His knees started to collapse.

Grabbing the tabletop to keep himself standing, he opened his mouth in a shrill howl of pain.

His eyes bulged and rolled in his head.

His face turned bright red.

Another painful howl escaped his throat. An animal howl. A *wolf* howl.

He clamped his eyes shut. He pounded the table with both hands. He tore at his white hair until it stood up in wild tufts.

His whole face twisted in agony.

And then, with an ugly groan from deep in his belly, he spun away from the table. And staggered to the door. Staggered like an animal, moaning and growling.

And vanished from the lab.

My heart throbbed. My chest ached. I realized I'd been holding my breath the whole time. I let it out in a loud whoosh.

I pushed open the cabinet door with my shoulder. And half fell, half leaped out of the narrow cabinet.

"I don't *believe* it," I murmured. "He *is* the beast. Uncle Jekyll *is* the creature."

My head spun. I raised both hands to my cheeks. My skin was burning hot!

What can I do? I asked myself.

Who can I tell?

I've got to stop him. I've got to get help for him.

But who can help?

I couldn't think clearly. I couldn't think of anything at all.

I kept seeing the tortured expression on Uncle Jekyll's face. And hearing the animal howls that burst from his throat.

I stared at the empty test tubes lying on their sides on the table. How could he drink that stuff? *How?*

I've got to get out of here, I decided.

I turned to the door — and screamed.

Uncle Jekyll stood inside the doorway.

He had returned to the lab!

He was breathing hard, grunting with each breath, staring at me. Staring angrily.

"Heidi," he growled. "I'm so sorry you saw."

He lumbered towards me, his eyes rolling
wildly.

"Wh-what are you going to do?" I stammered.
I backed away from him, backed up until I hit
the metal cabinets.

He grunted in reply. And grabbed my arm
with both hands.

"Uncle Jekyll — stop!" I cried. "What are you
doing?"

"Sorry you saw," he rasped again. His chest
heaved up and down. His breath came in hoarse
wheezes.

"Let go!" I pleaded.

But his grip tightened, and he pulled me
away from the cabinets. I tried to pull back, but
he was too strong.

He dragged me from the lab. Up the stairs.
And pushed me into my room.

I spun round to face him. "Why are you doing
this?" I cried.

He lurched into the hall and slammed the bedroom door shut. I heard the lock click.

I dived for the door. "Uncle Jekyll — I can help you! Let me help you! Don't lock me in here. Why are you doing this?"

"For your own good," he replied in a hoarse animal growl.

I heard his heavy footsteps going down the stairs.

I tried the door. Locked. He'd locked me in.

"Uncle Jekyll—" I called.

I knew he couldn't hear me. I heard the front door slam.

I ran to the bedroom window and peered out into the darkness.

After a few seconds, he staggered into view. I took a deep breath and tried to slow my racing heart as I watched him make his way down the hill towards the village. After a minute or so, he disappeared into the shadows.

"Why?" I murmured, shaking my head. "Why?"

Does he plan to keep me locked up in here for ever? I asked myself.

No. He can't.

And then I thought of an even more frightening question: what does he plan to do with me when he gets back?

Through the open window, I heard a shrill

scream. And then frightened shouts from down the hill.

"I have to get out of here," I told myself.

I tried tugging the doorknob with all my strength. Then I tried to batter the door open with my shoulder.

No way. The door was solid oak.

I dived to the window. I heard more screams from town. Flames shot up. More angry cries. A siren wailed.

I leaned out of the window and looked down. A two-storey drop straight to the ground. No tree to climb down. No shrubs below to break my fall.

"I can't jump out," I decided. "I'll break my neck."

Then I spotted the metal rain gutter at the corner of the house. Rusted, its paint peeling, it ran along the roof, then straight down nearly to the ground.

If I can wrap my hands around it, I can slide down, I decided. But will it hold my weight?

Only one way to find out.

I leaned further out the window and reached for it . . . reached. . .

No. It was just centimetres from my grasp. I couldn't lean any further. I couldn't reach it.

Wait, I thought. I ducked back into the room and pulled the desk chair to the window. My legs trembling, I climbed on to it. Then I leaned out of the window again.

Reached . . . reached for the gutter.

My fingers brushed the rusted metal—

—and then I lost my balance.

I felt my body plunging forward . . . plunging out of the window. . .

. . .and I fell.

I screamed — and grabbed wildly for the gutter.

My hands wrapped round it. The rusted metal scraped my skin.

I cried out and held on. Sliding . . . sliding too fast.

The pain grew too intense.

My hands flew off the gutter.

I landed hard on my back.

I didn't feel the landing. I didn't feel anything.

My wind was knocked out of me. I gasped for breath.

I'm dying, I thought.

But then I pulled in a wheezing breath. And, ignoring the pain, forced it out.

Above me, the house came back into view. And above it, the sky, pink with a high blanket of grey clouds.

I sucked in another breath. Another. The air felt so cool.

I began to feel again. Felt the snow on the back of my neck. Felt the cold dampness of the ground through my clothes.

My hands throbbed and burned, burned from sliding on the rusted metal gutter.

I sat up.

And heard a scream. And sirens down the hill.

"Uncle Jekyll—" I choked out.

I climbed unsteadily to my feet. The ground rocked and bobbed beneath me. I shut my eyes, waiting for my legs to stop trembling.

"I'm okay," I murmured. I bent down and rubbed cold snow on my burning hands.

Then I began jogging down the hill.

What did I plan to do when I reached the village?

I didn't know. I couldn't think clearly. But I had nowhere else to run.

Maybe I can save Uncle Jekyll, I thought.

A deafening explosion made me stop. Somewhere in the village a mountain of flames burst up like a volcano erupting.

Shrill screams and cries rose up over the roar of the flames. In the flickering yellow-orange light, I could see people running frantically in all directions.

Maybe I can pull Uncle Jekyll away from there, I thought.

I instantly realized it was a crazy idea.

He was a *beast* now, an inhuman creature.

He had to be stopped.

Breathing hard, I reached the edge of the village. I heard the crack of gunshots. I ran past an overturned car, its tyres spinning.

I turned on to the main street. Police officers patrolled, guns out, ready for action. In the orange light of the fires, their faces were grim and angry.

"Get away from here!" a man shouted.

It took me a few seconds to realize he was shouting at me.

"Stay out of town!"

"The beast is angry tonight!"

"Get off the street!"

Their shouts rang out over the crackling of the fires, the wail of sirens, the terrified screams. They hurried away, towards a burning house on the next corner.

I turned, eager to get off the street.

Too late.

"Noooooo!" I uttered a shocked scream as the creature leaped out from the side of a house.

A wolf! A snarling wolf-creature, howling, snapping his wet jaws. His grey-and-brown fur bristling. Lumbering forward stiffly on two legs.

His red eyes glowed and then locked on me.

I backed across a snow-covered lawn. Too late to run.

Too late to hide.

The growling creature moved quickly, arching his body for the attack.

I searched frantically for a weapon. A stick. A tree branch. Something to use to bat it away.

No. Nothing.

With a hideous roar, the beast spread his furry arms — and dived for me.

With a terrified cry, I dropped to the ground. My face plunged into the hard-packed snow.

I jerked my head up in time to see the beast sail over me.

I tried to scramble away.

But before I could climb to my feet, I felt a heavy paw on my back.

"No!" I gasped.

Grunting loudly, the beast pushed me down. Held me down on the snow.

"Uncle Jekyll—" I choked out. "Please. . ."

I turned and saw him tilt up his head and send an animal roar to the sky.

And then I saw a figure come running across the street.

Aaron!

Yes. Aaron. Waving a baseball bat in front of him with both hands.

"Heidi — run!" he cried breathlessly. Flames

from a burning car lit up his face, and I could see the fear on his twisted features. "Run!"

"I . . . can't!" I gasped. "The beast — he has me pinned down."

Aaron came running, swinging the bat furiously.

The beast let go of me. Roaring angrily, he rose on to his hind legs and spun round to face Aaron.

"It's my uncle!" I cried to Aaron. "The beast is my uncle! I saw him drink a chemical and—"

Another angry roar drowned out my words.

"Run!" Aaron cried shrilly, his dark eyes reflecting the firelight. "The people — the people of the village are going to destroy him! We can't take it any more! They plan to go up the hill, Heidi. They plan to burn down your uncle's house!"

"No!" I gasped.

And then my cry was cut short as the beast shoved me roughly aside.

Aaron swung the baseball bat.

The beast grabbed it from Aaron's hands — and flung it across the snow.

I screamed again as the snarling creature leaped at Aaron.

The beast picked Aaron up easily in both hairy paws. Lifted him high in the air.

And threw him into the fire.

My entire body locked in horror as I watched Aaron disappear into the flames.

I forced myself to move. Forced myself to run to the fire to help him.

But the beast blocked my path. Clawed at me. Swung a huge, powerful arm. His sharp claws sliced through my jacket.

He swiped again, aiming for my face.

I dived to the ground, sprawling on to my elbows and knees.

Climbing up, I saw Aaron come scrambling out of the fire. He rolled in the snow. Rolled over and over.

And then jumped to his feet. "I'm okay, Heidi!" he called to me, cupping his hands round his mouth. "Run!"

I gazed at him for a moment, making sure he wasn't burned. Making sure he really was okay.

The snarling beast lurched at me again.

The creature dived with such fury, he lost his balance. He slipped to his knees in the snow.

And I took off.

I ran past the burning car, past houses with their windows shattered, past a speeding patrol car, its siren blaring. Then I headed up the hill.

Why was I returning to the house?

I had nowhere else to run.

Halfway up the hill, I turned back.

And to my horror, I saw the snarling beast following me.

"Ohhhhh." A terrified moan escaped my throat.

Now what? Now what?

I couldn't think.

I burst into the house, my chest heaving, my throat aching. The dark hall spun before me.

Where to go? Where can I hide? Is there any place I will be safe?

I'll hide until the potion wears off, I decided. Yes! Maybe the potion will wear off. And then I can talk to Uncle Jekyll, try to reason with him.

Maybe. . . Maybe I can convince him to send me somewhere safe.

But where?

This is my home now.

My home. . .

But not for long. The villagers will soon be coming to burn it down!

And then what?

Too many thoughts. I squeezed my hands against my head. My brain felt ready to explode!

I heard a low growl from outside. In my terror, I had left the front door wide open!

He'll be in here any second. I've got to hide — now! I decided.

I spun away from the door and went running through the hall. The door to my uncle's lab stood open, all the lights on.

I burst inside, panting, my side aching.

I glanced around frantically, searching for a hiding place.

Should I go back into the cabinet? Would he find me there?

My eyes stopped at the lab table — and another crazy idea flashed into my head.

Drink the potion, Heidi, I told myself.

Drink the same potion your uncle drank — and become a beast too. If you don't, you won't stand a chance. It's the only way you can fight him.

Was it a crazy idea? Or a brilliant idea?

I didn't have time to decide. I heard the beast's heavy footsteps in the hall.

I lurched to the table. Grabbed the test tube. And raised it to my lips.

Empty.

The test tube was empty.

I shook it. I peered into it.

Of *course* it was empty. I had watched Uncle Jekyll drink it down.

I grabbed the one beside it. He had drunk from both of them. The second one was empty too.

It fell from my hand as the beast swept into the lab. His fur-covered feet thudded wetly over the floor. He pulled his dark lips back, baring jagged wolf-teeth.

"Uncle Jekyll—" I choked out, backing away.

His red eyes locked on mine. Teeth still bared, he uttered a low animal grunt.

And stepped towards me.

"Uncle Jekyll — it's me — Heidi," I called in a shrill, quivering voice. "Do you recognize me? Do you know me?"

The beast grunted again in reply.

"You wouldn't hurt me, would you?" I cried. "Please. You wouldn't hurt your own niece — would you?"

He opened his jaws in an angry roar and swiped a paw angrily in front of him.

Waving his arm in front of him, as if clearing a path, he moved towards me, snarling, grunting, wheezing.

I backed up against the wall.

Trapped. Nowhere to run.

He moved in slowly, steadily. Growling sharply now. Snapping his jaws. A white froth bubbled over his lips.

I raised my hands in front of me, trying to shield myself.

The beast raised both arms to attack.

And then I heard a sound behind him. A sound from the lab door.

The beast stopped — and turned away from me.

I gaped over his furry shoulder — and saw a figure hurry into the lab.

Uncle Jekyll!

"Heidi—" Uncle Jekyll cried from the doorway. "Are you okay?"

I opened my mouth to reply — but no sound came out.

Uncle Jekyll?

Trembling all over, I gazed from the growling beast to Uncle Jekyll.

I was wrong! I realized to my shock.

Uncle Jekyll *isn't* the beast!

The creature raked a paw at Uncle Jekyll, as if warning him away. Then it turned to me, opened its jaws in an angry roar, and hunched its shoulders, preparing to pounce.

Uncle Jekyll leaped across the room. He tackled the snarling creature from behind. Wrapped his arms round its waist and wrestled it . . . wrestled it away from me.

The beast struggled to free itself, thrashing its furry arms, bending its knees, heaving its shoulders.

But Uncle Jekyll held on tight. Hugging the angry creature . . . hugging it . . . hugging it. . .

Until the beast surrendered. Stopped its struggles.

With a long sigh, the creature lowered its head and shut its eyes. Its shoulders slumped. Its whole body sagged.

And still Uncle Jekyll held on, hugging it, hugging it so tightly, I wondered if it could breathe.

And as my uncle hugged it, pressing his head against the furry back, the creature began to change.

To shrink. . .

The fur pulled back into the skin.

The light faded from the blazing red eyes. The frothing snout melted into the face.

As I stared in silent shock, the beast shrunk . . . hunched in on itself. . .

And when it raised its head, it had turned back into — Marianna!

Her black curls fell wetly, covering her face. Her shoulders heaved up and down. She pressed her face against her father's chest. And cried softly.

Uncle Jekyll held her tightly. And raised his sad, red-rimmed eyes to me. "Heidi, I locked you in your room to keep you safe," he said, his voice just above a whisper. "I warned you to stay there. I didn't want you to get involved."

"I . . . I tried to help," I stammered, still staring in shock at Marianna. Marianna the Beast. "Uncle Jekyll, I didn't know. . ." The words caught in my throat.

Marianna raised her head. Tears rolled down her swollen cheeks. "Daddy," she whispered. "What am I going to do?"

Uncle Jekyll patted her hair gently. "I don't know, Marianna," he replied. "I spend all my time trying to find a cure for you. You know I'm here in the lab, working on it night and day."

A sob escaped Marianna's throat. "I can't go on like this, Dad. Being a person in the daytime . . . and a creature at night."

"I know, I know," Uncle Jekyll said softly. "Some day soon, I will find the right cure. If I just keep trying. I drink it myself. I test each one on myself to see what it does. You know that I'll do anything to find the right mixture to keep you from transforming."

I swallowed hard. "Uncle Jekyll, how did this happen?" I asked quietly. "Why does this happen to Marianna?"

He uttered a sigh. "It happened five years ago. Marianna was seven. We were travelling in Europe. Our car broke down in the middle of a forest."

He sighed again. "I remember it so clearly," he said, still hugging Marianna. "She got bored while the car was being fixed. She wandered

101

into the forest and got lost. When I finally found her..."

He swallowed a sob. "When I finally found Marianna, she told me about a forest creature. It attacked her. It bit her. I didn't know whether to believe her or not. She was always making up stories."

He gently patted Marianna's hair. "One bite of the creature was all it took to ruin Marianna's life. A few weeks later, Marianna transformed for the first time. And now, most nights, she transforms into a frightening, angry beast. I . . . I've been searching for a cure ever since. I think I'm close, but—"

He stopped.

Marianna raised her head, suddenly alert.

All three of us heard the angry shouts. The thud of boots on the hill.

"No!" Uncle Jekyll let out a scream as a rock came crashing through the lab window.

And then we heard the steady chant from the villagers outside. "Kill the beast . . . kill the beast . . . kill the beast!"

"Kill the beast . . . kill the beast. . ."

The sound of the ugly chant burst through the shattered window.

"Burn it down!" someone shouted. "Burn the house down!"

We heard people battering the front door. And more wild, angry shouts:

"Burn the house!"

"First, kill the beast!"

"Kill the evil!"

Another rock sailed into the lab. It hit a shelf of beakers on the wall. Shattered glass flew across the room.

Uncle Jekyll's eyes bulged wide in fear. He still had his arms round Marianna. But she pulled away in panic, lurched towards the lab door, then turned back. "Dad — what do we do?"

Uncle Jekyll uttered a long, sad sigh. He stared at the broken window.

"Kill the beast . . . kill the beast. . ." The angry chants grew louder. The pounding on the front door sounded like booms of thunder.

"Are we trapped in here?" I cried, shouting over the wild cries and chanting voices. "They're out of control. They'll kill us all!"

Uncle Jekyll grabbed my hand and pulled me towards Marianna at the door. "I planned for this," he said. "We can escape. But we have to be fast."

We ran into the passage. And heard a loud cracking sound.

"The front door!" I gasped. "They've broken it down."

"This way!" Uncle Jekyll cried.

He led us along the back corridor. We turned a corner into a narrow passage I'd never seen.

I heard angry cries. From inside the house! Heavy footsteps.

I smelled smoke. "They're setting the house on fire!" I cried.

Uncle Jekyll pulled open a narrow door. "In here," he instructed. He moved aside. Marianna and I stepped inside.

Uncle Jekyll pulled the door closed behind us. A steep staircase led down to the basement. Our shoes thudded on the creaking stairs as we made our way down.

"They'll search for us. They'll find us down

here," Marianna whispered to her father. "If they burn the house, we'll be trapped."

Uncle Jekyll raised a finger to his lips. His eyes were narrowed in determination. Ducking his head under the low ceiling, he guided us through the cluttered basement. Past the enormous, chugging, vibrating furnace. Past a storage area piled high with wooden boxes and old steamer trunks.

He picked up a torch on a worktable and clicked it on. Then we followed the darting beam of light through two large, empty spaces, our footsteps echoing on the concrete floor. And stopped at a tall wooden crate against the far wall.

"Help me," Uncle Jekyll instructed. He leaned his shoulder against the crate and started to push. Marianna and I moved to the other side and pulled.

Above us, I heard heavy footsteps. Angry shouts. The villagers were searching the house.

The crate slid a centimetre at a time. Finally, we moved it far enough to reveal a low opening in the basement wall.

"It's a tunnel," Uncle Jekyll said, wiping sweat from his forehead with his coat sleeve. "An escape tunnel."

I peered into the low, dark opening. "Where does it lead?"

"It goes down the hill. Past the village,"

Uncle Jekyll replied. "It ends less than two kilometres from the road. We'll be safe. And maybe we can hitch a ride to somewhere far away."

A loud crash upstairs made me jump. The sharp smell of smoke drifted down through the basement ceiling.

"Hurry," Uncle Jekyll urged. "We want to be out of the tunnel before they search the basement."

I ducked my head and stepped into the narrow opening. My eyes adjusted slowly to the darkness. Uncle Jekyll aimed the torch at our feet.

The tunnel was concrete, low and round, cut into the hill. I heard the scuttle of tiny feet up ahead. Field mice? Racoons? Rats?

No time to worry about them.

Hunching low, we began making our way through the tunnel. It curved slowly and then began to slope down. The circle of light from the torch danced on the floor ahead of us.

No one spoke. The only sounds now were the scrape of our shoes on the tunnel floor and our rapid, shallow breathing.

I kept listening for footsteps behind us. But the villagers hadn't discovered the tunnel yet.

After a minute or two, I stopped.

"Whoa. Wait," I called. My voice echoed off the low walls.

"What's wrong?" Uncle Jekyll demanded. "We have a long way to go, Heidi."

"I know," I replied. "But I have to go back. I forgot something."

"No — you can't!" Marianna cried out, her voice trembling in fright. "They'll capture you. They'll *kill* you!"

"What did you forget?" Uncle Jekyll demanded. "It can't be important enough to—"

"It's a diary," I told him. "A very old diary."

"No, Heidi—" my uncle started.

But I didn't give him a chance to finish. I turned away from them and took off, back towards the basement.

I knew that going back up to the house was crazy. But the old diary was too valuable to leave behind. It was probably worth a fortune. And it was part of history.

I couldn't let it burn with the rest of the house. I couldn't let such an important document be lost for ever.

I had to rescue it.

"Heidi — come back!" Uncle Jekyll's cry rang out through the tunnel, far behind me now.

I turned a corner, and the tunnel opening came into view. I hunched under the low ceiling and stepped into the basement.

Thick smoke choked my throat. I heard shouts upstairs. Running footsteps.

I took a deep breath and held it. Then,

pressing my hand over my nose and mouth, I made my way to the basement stairs.

Could I get up to my room?

Could I rescue the old diary from its secret hiding place — and make my escape again?

I had to try.

Clouds of thick, sour smoke billowed around me. Holding my breath, my eyes stinging, I ran to the stairs.

I hesitated at the top of the stairs and listened. Were there villagers on the other side of the door?

My lungs were bursting. I couldn't stay there. I had to breathe.

I pushed open the basement door and stepped into the back corridor. Letting my breath out in a *whoosh,* I peered up and down the hall.

I heard angry shouts from the front of the house. The crackle of flames.

I pressed myself against the wall as a group of men in the next passage thundered by. Holding my breath again, I waited until they ran out of sight. Then, keeping close to the wall, I began inching my way to the front staircase.

As I passed the kitchen, I saw two men with

axes, furiously chopping away at the sink and worktops.

"Destroy everything!" someone shouted.

"This is what he did to our town!" someone else cried.

"Where is he? Don't let him escape!"

"Did anyone search the roof?"

"Is there a basement?"

The curtains in the study were on fire. Flames leaped up from the sofa.

In the living room a group of boys about my age were smashing the front window. Tearing apart the furniture.

I backed into a cupboard as two men ran past carrying flaming torches.

"Where is the beast?"

"He didn't go far!"

"He won't leave this house!"

Their angry words stabbed at me like knives.

You don't know the truth, I thought bitterly. You don't know that Marianna is the beast. That she can't help herself. You don't know how hard my uncle is working to find a cure. To rid the village of the beast.

But that didn't matter now. Uncle Jekyll and Marianna would never be able to return to the village. Never be able to return to their house.

The house will be destroyed before the villagers leave, I realized.

110

An explosion of bright flames lit up the hall.

I peered out from the cupboard. The coast was clear.

I lurched to the stairs, and leaning forward, I began running up them at full speed.

Please, please, let me get to my bedroom, I prayed.

Let me find the hidden diary. And let me return to the tunnel, return to Marianna and Uncle Jekyll.

Then I never want to see this village again.

I reached the top of the stairs, breathing hard. I could hear cries and shouts in Marianna's room at the end of the hall.

A loud crash made me gasp. They were destroying her room too.

I darted into my room. The room looked as if a tornado had swept through it. My drawers had been pulled out and tossed on to the floor. My clothes had been strewn everywhere.

The window curtains had been ripped off their rod. The window smashed. Glass everywhere.

I didn't care.

I dived for the bookshelf. Pulled down the board over the hidden compartment.

Was the old diary still inside?

Yes.

I grabbed it with a trembling hand. My hand shook so hard, I nearly dropped it.

Glancing over my shoulder to the door, I tucked the diary into my coat pocket.

I took one last glance at the room and then, with a shudder, made my way back to the hall.

I stopped when I heard excited voices in the next room.

"Is there an attic? There has to be an attic."

"If he's hiding up there, we'll find him."

I turned and began running to the stairs. I could feel the diary bouncing in my pocket.

I stopped at the top of the stairs. Peered down. No one there.

I reached for the banister.

And strong hands grabbed me from behind.

I turned to see two men, eyes wild, wet hair matted to their heads, sweat running down their faces.

"I've got one!" one of them cried, gripping my shoulder tightly.

"Yes!" the other cheered. "We've got one!" He lowered his sweating face to me. "Lead us to the beast!" he snarled. "Lead us to the beast now — or your life is over!"

"No—" I screamed. I struggled to squirm out of their grasp.

But they were too strong.

"Tell us where the beast is!" one of them growled, squeezing my arm. "Tell us now, and we'll let you go."

"But — I don't know!" I cried. "I just moved here. I . . . I really don't know what you're talking about!"

The two men narrowed their eyes at me, studying me suspiciously.

"She's lying," one of them snapped.

"Tell us the truth," his partner demanded, spitting the words in my face. "Tell us the truth or you'll never leave this house!"

"Let her go!" a voice called.

All three of us turned to see Aaron running down the passage.

"Let her go!" he told them again. "She doesn't

know anything. I met her at the bus station on Monday. She's just arrived here."

The two men ignored Aaron. One of them let go of my arm. But he didn't back away. "Have you seen the beast? Where is he hiding?" he shouted.

"Tell us!" his friend demanded again.

Flames crackled behind them. Angry shouts rang out through the house.

"I — I don't know," I stammered. "I really don't know."

Aaron grabbed my hand. "I'm taking her out of here. Can't you see she's telling the truth?" He pulled me away.

We started to run. Thick, sour smoke swirled through the hall. My eyes watering, I glanced back. The two men hadn't moved. They weren't following us.

"We've got to get out fast," Aaron cried. "They're going to destroy the whole house. They won't stop until they capture your uncle."

"This way." I tugged him through the back hall. Then down the basement stairs.

Our shoes thudded over the concrete floor. I led Aaron to the tunnel, and we burst inside it. Then, running hard, we followed it as it sloped down the hill.

I kept glancing back, praying that no one was following us.

We seemed to run for ever. I was breathing

hard, my side aching, when we finally climbed out the other end.

"Uncle Jekyll? Marianna?" I called their names breathlessly.

No sign of them.

Did they escape to safety?

Did they get away?

Would I ever see them again?

So many frantic questions ran through my mind.

Pulling my wet hair off my forehead, I gazed around. The tunnel had led us past the village, to a row of low hills that faced the road.

The village stood quiet and empty behind the low hills. I turned, struggling to catch my breath.

In the distance, high above the village, I could see a wall of orange-and-yellow flames, so bright, so bright against the purple night sky.

The flames appeared to reach up to the moon.

Uncle Jekyll's house. Burning . . . burning to the ground. The heat and smoke swept down the hill. Washcd over Aaron and me.

My eyes welled with tears. The heat and smoke stung my face.

But I didn't move. I stared up at the house, watching it burn, watching it vanish in the raging flames . . . until Aaron gently pulled me away.

Later, we sat in Aaron's kitchen. His mother gave us dinner. She said I could stay with them until we contacted my other relatives.

Outside, we could hear the villagers returning from the hill. I knew they had to be unhappy. They destroyed Uncle Jekyll's house, but they didn't capture the beast.

I trembled, picturing the fire, the wall of flames reaching up to the sky. I wondered if Uncle Jekyll and Marianna were somewhere safe.

Yes. They had to be. By now, they were far away from here.

The horror was over. . .

"Hey!" I suddenly remembered the diary.

"Aaron, I have to show you something," I said. I hurried to the cupboard, pulled the diary from my coat pocket, then returned to the kitchen.

Aaron stared at the little book. "What's that?"

"This is why I went back to the house," I told him excitedly. "It's an old diary. I found it hidden in my bedroom. I think it's very valuable. I think it's the diary of the original Dr Jekyll."

"Huh?" Aaron's mouth dropped open. "Let me see that."

He took the diary from my hand and examined the worn, faded cover. Then he started to skim through it, squinting at the tiny handwriting.

"Whoa. Heidi?" He raised his eyes to me. "It's not an old diary. Check this out."

He handed it up to me, open to one of the first pages. I read it out loud:

"This diary is the property of Marianna Jekyll."

I let out a gasp. "I didn't see this page," I told Aaron. "So it's Marianna's diary! Wow! She used a faded, old diary. But the entries were new."

When did she stop writing in it? I wondered. I flipped through the pages until I found the last entry in the book.

Then I brought the diary close to my face and started to read.

As I read Marianna's words, I froze, gripped in horror, gripped in the fear that *my* horror was only beginning:

. . .I hid the diary in my cousin Heidi's room. I never want anyone to find it. I never want anyone to know my shame, to know what I have done. I was out of control . . . that is my only excuse.

Soon after Heidi arrived, I was a creature. I was not myself. I crept into Heidi's room to write in my diary. I saw her sleeping there. I had no control. She slept so soundly . . . I leaned over her bed . . . I BIT her shoulder . . . bit her . . . bit her. . .

117

Trembling, I raised my eyes to find Aaron staring hard at me.

"Heidi — what's wrong?" he asked. "Why do you look so strange?"

Welcome to the new millennium of fear

Check out this chilling preview
of what's next from
R. L. Stine

Scream School

"You're coming to my house for dinner, right?" Carlos asked, dribbling at the foul line

"Yeah. And we'll watch a film?" Jake answered, bending over to catch his breath.

Jake loved going over to Carlos's house. His parents had their own screening room with a projector and full-size screen. And they had the most amazing collection of old horror films.

Carlos and Jake loved to watch the classic black-and-white films: *Bride of Frankenstein, The Wolfman, The Invisible Man.*

The two of them screamed their heads off, even though the old films seemed kind of funny now.

One day, Jake told his dad how much he enjoyed the old horror films.

"Great old stuff," Emory replied. "If you ever get too scared while you're watching, just remind yourself that it's only a film."

Jake dribbled the ball past Carlos. Carlos

slapped at it and missed. Jake went up for his shot.

"Hey, Jake —" A voice from the driveway.

Jake turned. Missed the shot. The ball hit the rim and bounced away.

Chelsea came running over, her light-brown hair flying behind her. She wore a white tennis outfit and carried a tennis racket. "What are you guys doing?" she asked.

"Knitting a sweater," Jake replied. He was still angry that she had laughed at him at dinner the night before. "What does it look like we're doing?"

Chelsea pretended to hit him on the head with her tennis racket. "I meant, are you playing a game or just messing around?"

"Both," Carlos replied, grinning. "Want to play? How about Jake and me against you?"

"No way," Chelsea replied. She set her racket down on the grass beside the court. "Basketball isn't my sport. I kind of stink at it."

"Okay. You and Jake against me," Carlos suggested. "I'll try to go easy on you two."

They started their game. Chelsea tried to dribble the ball past Carlos, who danced in front of her, waving both hands in her face.

"Pass it! Pass it!" Jake cried.

Chelsea dribbled to the basket. Shot and scored.

"Lucky shot," Carlos murmured.

He took the ball out. Started to dribble, dancing to one side, then the other. Fancy footwork.

Showing off for Chelsea, Jake thought.

Chelsea moved in front of Carlos — and stole the ball from his hands. She dribbled, backing over the half-court line, then moved forward.

"Pass it! Here!" Jake called, waving his arms over his head. "I'm open!"

Chelsea ignored him and fired off a two-handed layup. It swished through the basket. "Four to zip," she told Carlos.

"Hey — am I in this game or what?" Jake complained.

"Know what Jake did yesterday on his dad's film set?" Chelsea asked Carlos. She cast a mischievous, teasing glance at Jake.

"No, what?" Carlos asked, dribbling in place.

"Shut up, Chelsea!" Jake snapped. "Just shut up!"

"What did he do?" Carlos asked, grinning at Chelsea.

Chelsea opened her mouth to reply.

But all three of them froze when they heard the loud growls. And saw the enormous black rottweiler come roaring into the yard.

The ball fell out of Carlos's hands and rolled away.

"Oh, no . . . I know this dog," Jake moaned, backing up.

Barking furiously, the huge dog lowered its head, preparing to attack.

"No, Dukie! No!" Jake pleaded. He raised both hands, trying to shield himself. "Dukie — down! Down!"

The dog opened its jaws in a furious growl.

"Oh . . . help!" Jake cried as the dog raised its front paws. Leaped heavily on to him. Knocked Jake to the ground.

And lowered its massive head to attack.